Cupcakes and Conspiracy

The Cupcake Capers Prequel

POLLY HOLMES

Western Australia

Copyright

This book is a work of fiction. The names, characters, places and incidents are products of the writer's imagination or have been used fictitiously and are not to be constructed as real. Any resemblance to persons, living or dead, actual events, local or organisations is entirely coincidental.

From the Author

For years, stories full of deliciously twisted mysteries have been living rent-free in my head, whispering clues, motives, and mayhem at all hours. There's something irresistible about a good murder mystery—the tension, the clever reveals, the satisfaction of watching all the crumbs (or cupcake sprinkles) fall perfectly into place. Crafting those puzzles has always been a joy, and returning to the very beginning of this world feels like rediscovering why I fell in love with it in the first place.

This prequel isn't just another book; it's a chance to explore the origins of the chaos, charm, and crime-solving that made Cupcake Capers so special.

This book has been written by me personally. It has been professionally edited, proofread, and carefully beta read, but the odd typo may still have slipped past—humans do miss things from time to time. If you spot anything, feel free to send it through to pollyholmes@pollyholmesmysteries.com and I'll make sure it's sorted.

Enough of my rambling. From here on out, the trouble is baked in and ready to rise. Let the delicious chaos begin.

Love

Polly

xxooxxxooo

Also by Polly Holmes

The Cupcake Capers - Culinary
Prequel - Cupcakes and Conspiracy
Cupcakes and Cyanide #1
Cupcakes and Curses #2
Cupcakes and Corpses #3
Murder and Mistletoe #4
Dead Velvet Cupcakes #5

Melting Pot Café - Paranormal
Pumpkin Pies & Potions #1
Happy Deadly New Year #2
Muffins & Magic #3
Mistletoe, Murder & Mayhem #4
A Deadly Disappearance Down Under # 5
Black Magic Murder #6
Cupcakes & Cauldrons #7
One Hex Too Many #8
An Act of Murder #9
Meringues, Matrimony & Murder #10
Cats, Crime & Crème Brulée – Novella

Polly Holmes writing as
P.L. Harris

The Well Watchers of Breckin River - Paranormal Romantic Suspense

The Secret Legacy #1

The Secret Grimoire #2

The Secret Curse #3

The Secret Princess #4

The Secret Society #5

Dedication

For all the cozy mystery lovers out there.

Chapter One

THE SICKLY SWEET scent of jasmine pierced the thick layer of tension coating the Town Hall. Betty Brookson leant back in her chair and gazed at her friends, her family, her home. Most only get one chance at happiness in life. She was blessed. She had two. The Ashton Point community welcomed her with open arms when she and Bob married all those years ago and now, their peaceful seaside town was under threat of destruction. She swallowed hard as nausea kept rising in the back of her throat.

Over my old decrepit dead body.

Running her sweaty palms down her slacks, she held on to her control. Just. Bob would turn in his grave at the injustice that lay before them. A concrete high-rise apartment block where the nursing home stands. How could they?

Mr Collins stood at the lectern visibly shaking. He looked frazzled by the continuous holler of questions and abuse directed his way. He held his trembling hands up in a placative manner. "N…now, if you would all calm down, I'm sure I can answer all your questions in due time."

Silence was no longer an option. Betty's belly twisted and turned. Rising from her chair, her exterior projected a picture of serene calmness. Her gaze zeroed in on the big wig corporate executive at the back of the stage fiddling with his phone. Their desperate pleas ignored.

"Thank you, Mr Collins but I would like to direct my questions directly to Mr Pantell," Betty said, her aging back stiffening. Her ears pricked. The unnerving mummers across the room fuelled her voice. With one hand she held the back of the chair in front and with the other she gripped her elbow crutch. Her gaze dropped to her bandaged ankle. Pressed to the floor good as new.

See? I don't even need this damn thing anymore. My foot works perfectly. I'm old, not a cripple.

The stocky man's eyes thinned as he approached the lectern. His black mullet a bad attempt at matching the sexy style of Mel Gibson. He shoved Mr Collins aside and cleared his throat. A high-pitched nasal tone assaulted her ears.

"Yes, madam? Is there something you wanted to say?"

Betty paused, shocked at his feminine voice and barely able to keep her laughter hidden.

"Do you have a burning question to ask, or not? None of us are getting any younger, including yourself."

Gasps and ripples of disgust from annoyed town folk filled the room. Pain shot in her palm as her nails dug in when she gripped the handle of the elbow crutch tighter. A small gasp left her lips. It was squeeze hard or throw it at the arrogant, patronising jerk.

Pursing her lips into a thin line, she continued. "Do you even care you're putting the aged out on the street? The nursing home is a much-needed facility. Just because we're old doesn't mean we don't need help. The elderly has a voice, a voice that will stand together, and…Will…Be…Heard?" She staccatoed her last three words. For impact.

A booming roar of support erupted from the packed town hall.

"Here, here…"

"…You tell 'em, Betty…"

"Take your crappy development somewhere else. We don't want it!"

Instant pride warmed Betty's heart. As quickly as it came, it squashed with a sudden stab of grief. Bob should have been standing by her side in this fight. Tears welled in her eyes. Losing him six months ago was akin to losing half of herself. A wretched time of her life she'd never wish on her worst enemy. Even Helena Adams. An icy shiver tip-toed its way up her spine as she spotted her arch nemesis on the other side of the room.

They'd been friends. Once.

The high-pitched nasal drone blared through the speakers. "Ladies and gentlemen, if I may say a few words."

Pantell's irritating smug persona grated on Betty's nerves like sharp nails scraping down a chalkboard.

He cleared his throat. Again. "We at STA Developments sympathise with you, but we've been extremely accommodating. We've met each of the building codes, not to mention the additional hoops your council insisted we jump through. Our goal is to make Ashton Point a better place. Progress is happening people and you can either embrace it or stand in its way and be bulldozed."

"Bulldozed?" Betty's feet shunted forward as if drawn like a hypnotised bull to a red flag. "Do you think we will stand by while you, as you say, bulldoze our town in the name of progress?" Betty's stomach revolted at his sinister laugh.

"Let me remind you, we're not the enemy here," he continued over the mutters and mumbles of angry and frustrated residents. "We secured the land fairly and we are well within our rights to build whatever we want on the land."

"And destroy our nursing home? You ogre," Helena yelled from the other side of the hall. "That's what you are, an ogre with an ugly green head and ears like oversized horns. You make Shrek look handsome." Her words were met with hearty laughter. "We should be here with pitchforks, maybe then you'll listen."

They hadn't always seen eye to eye, especially when it came to food and the Easter Cooking Competition, but for now, Helena made it back on Betty's Christmas card list.

Fuming, Betty held her metal crutch up as if warding off Pantell's words. "Mr—"

"Let me remind you," Derek butted in, raising the volume of his voice above the complaints from the floor. "We've relocated all residents to nearby nursing homes. No one will live on the streets. Now, I think I've been patient long enough and if I can finish by asking you all to be open minded to what STA Developments can offer Ashton Point. Thank you."

* * *

"For the love of God," Derek muttered under his breath as he moved toward the stage exit. "If these people knew what was good for them, they'd shut up and be thankful we're putting them on the map." He plastered on a fake smile and marched toward the town hall side entrance.

"Taking the coward's way out, hey, Pantell?"

Coward? Derek stopped mid-step. The raw anguish of the word triggered a myriad of memories. This same word blurted from his father's lips the very last time he stormed from his childhood home, never to return. He spun, hit by a damning glare shooting from the woman's eyes. He sucked in a deep lungful of stale air, compressing the raw emotions burning the edge of his lips.

"Mrs…" He paused and took in the dainty appearance of the elderly woman. Multiple crow's feet covered in a light smattering of make-up edged the sides of her temples. Her platinum-grey locks framing her delicate face projecting an image of experience and maturity. In her younger days he imagined she might have been a stunningly beautiful woman.

"Brookson… Betty Brookson," she said, her tone laced with determination.

"Mrs Brookson, I'd hardly call myself a coward considering I personally made the trip up from Sydney especially for this meeting today. I was open to discussions but clearly the people of this town have one objective in mind. Now, if you'll excuse me, I'm sure Mr Collins will take it from here."

"I'm sure he could. Run away and leave your little puppy dog to take the heat." Betty shifted toward him, her free arm swishing around like a samurai sword slicing silk. "What kind of men are women raising these days? Men who would destroy a facility so crucial to this town, and a place my late husband was instrumental in establishing."

Councilman Calderson lightly tapped Betty's forearm. "I believe we should continue this conversation after we've all calmed down. What do you say, Betty?"

Her head snapped to the right and she huffed in Calderson's direction. "Calm down? I will not calm down and I don't understand how you can stand by and let this atrocity happen?"

"You know the council tried everything, but our hands were tied. STA Developments purchased the land legally from Duncan Swain. We're in this predicament because of him. He's disappeared and even though we've tried, we have no way of locating him."

"So, you see Mrs Brookson, the decision has been made for you," Derek snapped, his jaw clenched tightly.

"This isn't the last you've heard from me, Mr Pantell," Betty said, waving her walking elbow crutch high in his direction.

He resumed his track to the exit, determined to make this happen sooner rather than later. Anything to get out of this god-forsaken hick town.

Betty called, "I promise I will do everything in my power to stop you. I will see this through to the end, not just for me, but for the people of Ashton Point and my beloved Bob."

I'd like to see you try.

He glanced back at the old woman, her reddened face a triumph in his books. "Make sure you use that walking aid to assist your injured leg there, I'd hate for you to be so worked up you hurt yourself further. Good day, Mrs Brookson."

He took pleasure in the old woman's shocked jaw dropped expression. He spun, ignoring all the protesting remarks of abuse as he stormed out.

Damn, I love my job.

Chapter Two

BETTY PLACED HER bone china teacup down on the coffee table. Reclining in her favourite armchair, she swapped the phone from ear to ear. "I can't believe the ignorance of that man, Laurel. He made me so angry I wanted to throttle him right there on the spot."

"You shouldn't let him get to you," Laurel said. Her stern tone a stiff reminder of her lost temper. "You know the doctor will tell you to watch your blood pressure."

Betty sighed, her eyelids drooping under the weight of Laurel's timely reminder. "I know, I know. But the dismissive tone he used was downright rude. He doesn't give a hoot about the nursing home or the people who live there."

"I'm hearing you loud and clear." Laurel cleared her throat. "I'm sorry I missed the meeting this morning, but I can't shake this darn cough and now my stomach has decided to join the sick party."

A pang hit Betty square in the chest. Was her best friend okay? "Are you sure you're up for coming over to dinner tonight? We can postpone."

"Pfft, I'll be there. I'm not missing a chance to taste those award-winning cupcakes of yours." Laurel giggled, and it wasn't long before both women were in throes of happy laughter amidst a lengthy discussion about flour, honey and the current wool shop sale. "So, what time shall I be there?"

Betty glanced at the mahogany grandfather clock by the hallway entrance. "It's two o'clock now so how about we make it around six-thirty? I've got to pop into town to grab some ingredients. I'm testing a new secret recipe for the Easter competition. You'll be the first to try it and *if* it's as good as I think it is, there's no way Helena Adams will be able to beat me."

"They sound delicious. You're determined to be crowned Best Baker this year, aren't you?"

"You betcha. I had my appointment with Dr Harrison earlier today at the nursing home and he said I didn't need that silly walking crutch anymore.

There'll be no keeping me out of the kitchen now. You have no idea how frustrating it was relying on it."

"So, the foot's all better?" Laurel asked.

"Good as new," Betty said, holding up her strapped ankle. "Well, almost. As long as I promise to keep it strapped and rested for a few hours every day for the next two weeks. You know I'm a woman of her word."

"Wonderful. Let's hope you've learned your lesson. Trying to juggle all the shopping in one load from the car is *not* a good idea. I'll see you at six-thirty," Laurel said.

Betty smiled, a warm glow filling her chest. Spending the evening with her best friend was exactly what the doctor ordered. "Perfect. See you then."

* * *

Droplets of beaded sweat ran down Betty's neck from her damp hair. The hot oven had soared the temperature in the kitchen. "Mmmm," she said as she sucked in a lungful of the savoury scent. Disappointment gnawed at her when Laurel's illness forced her to cancel her evening visit, but Betty wasn't one to waste a perfectly good cooking opportunity.

She pulled a tray of muffins out of the oven and the kitchen filled with the succulent smell of warm blueberries. Ignoring the rising steam, she broke a corner off and popped it in her mouth, hot tingles biting her fingertips. Her eyelids closed. Heaven. Her tastebuds instantly thanked her for the luscious juicy mouthful. Which was more than she could say for her waistline. She only had to look at the damn muffins and it grew five inches.

I will beat you this year, Helena Adams. The Easter Cooking Competition crown will soon be mine once more.

She smiled and popped another piece in her mouth, her mind pre-occupied with the sinful taste. She didn't register the rattle of the doorbell.

* * *

Charlotte McCorrson heaved air into her lungs as she wiped threatening tears from her eyes with the heel of her palm. "God, men can be such pathetic human beings," she muttered as she took the freeway exit to Ashton Point. The evening sun sent a serene glow of lilac and pink feathering across the skyline as it faded.

She gripped the steering wheel as the icy air from the air-conditioner blew across her damp face, but it hadn't cooled her blazing insides. "How could I have been with such a jerk? A two-timing jerk. A married two-timing jerk at that."

Focus…deep breaths…Everything happens for a reason, or so Clair says.

Right now, she struggled to find the reason behind her blunder. Eager to escape embarrassment, she jumped in her car and high-tailed it to Ashton Point. Nothing soothed a broken heart like spending time with the best grandma in the world. She switched the air-conditioner off and wound down her window as she turned down Betty's street. She sucked in the salty air deep and shook the disastrous events of the morning from her head.

Charlotte gasped, and the air whooshed from her lungs at the sight before her.

What on earth is going on?

All thoughts of her tragic love life instantly forgotten. "Oh no, this can't be good." She pulled up behind the police car parked in Betty's driveway, its blue and red lights flashing like a Christmas Tree.

"Grandma...Grandma?" she yelled, as she barged through the front door making a beeline for the loungeroom. A stern heavy-set man with his arms folded across his chest blocked her path. She wasn't impressed by his tough-man impersonation of a nightclub bouncer, complete with grumpy frown. His harsh exterior resembled the Grouch from Sesame Street. If her memory served her correctly, he was Ashton Point's newest police detective.

He held his hands up, halting Charlotte mid-step. "Hold it young lady."

"What's going on and where is my grandma?" she demanded, her gaze drilling into him. Charlotte breathed a sigh of relief as she caught sight of Betty's cheeky smile peeking out from behind his shoulder. "Grandma, thank goodness. Are you okay?"

Betty stepped out and held her arms open. "Of course, I am. Charlotte, now come here and give your old grandmother a hug."

Charlotte eased herself forward and a cold hand clutched her heart as Detective Anderson thrust his hand out to ward her off. "Afraid I'll need you to wait there a moment. Your grandma is answering a few questions."

"Questions…about what?" She asked, her pulse racing, pain started throbbing against her temple.

"Detective Anderson here thinks I had something to do with the attack on Derek Pantell. Isn't that the most ridiculous thing you've ever heard?" Betty said, her words semi-hidden by a nervous laugh.

Charlotte's eyebrows raised. "Assault? My grandma assault someone? Who is Derek Pantell?"

A guttural rumble escaped his lips. "A visiting developer from Sydney. We work on evidence and at present all the evidence points to Betty."

Charlotte's jaw dropped. "You're serious, aren't you?"

"A brutal assault is no joking matter regardless how old the assailant may be," Detective Anderson said, turning his back on Charlotte. "Now, Betty, where were we?"

Brutal assault? As if.

Betty opened her mouth to speak but Charlotte scooted passed him, engulfing her in her arms. "Grandma, are you sure you're okay?"

"Now, listen here missy," Anderson spat, shaking a finger inches from her face. "I'd kindly ask you not to interfere in a police investigation."

Betty squeezed her tight. "Yes, darling girl, I'm fine."

Charlotte's gut cramped as she pulled back, running her eye cautiously up and down Betty's body. Her chest seized as her gaze landed on her strapped ankle. "What happened to your foot?"

Betty followed her gaze and chuckled. "This old injury? My stupidity, I'm afraid. The result of carrying all the shopping in from the car in one load. I tripped over a loose paver on the edge of the footpath. Nothing to worry about, dear. Dr Harrison said it's almost healed and I don't even need those annoying elbow crutches anymore."

Charlotte turned and gave her best death stare toward the frowning, pompous gentleman. "You say my grandma assaulted this Pantell guy, well where is he now? Did he see her attack him?"

His nostrils flared. "He's currently in a coma at Ashton Point Memorial Hospital under police guard and unless he's come around in the last hour, he's not telling us much at all."

The blood drained from her face. "A coma?"

Detective Anderson grunted in confirmation and flipped open his notebook. "Back to your crutches, where are they, Mrs Brookson?"

Dread gripped Charlotte's heart. "Why do you ask?"

Betty tutted and sighed. "I left them with Dr Harrison earlier today. He said as long as I keep it bandaged and with regular rest, I didn't need them anymore."

Charlotte repeated her question. "Again, why do you ask, Detective?"

"Not that it's any of your business," he muttered. "But it so happens a crutch was used in the assault on Mr Pantell."

Both women gasped in unison and heat rose in Charlotte's cheeks.

No, this can't be happening.

"An elbow crutch was found next to Mr Pantell covered in his blood and two sets of fingerprints, Mrs Brookson and Doc Harrison who, by the way, has an iron-clad alibi." He paused, pocketing his notebook, his harsh gaze focused on Betty. "I think it would be best if you accompany me to the station for further questioning." His brow creased, and he looked in pain as if he had a carrot stuck up his butt.

"You can't be serious?" Charlotte asked, the tension in her gut ready to explode. "Do you have any other evidence against my grandma? Like for instance, did anyone see her near the scene of the crime?"

He shook his head. "We haven't found any witness at this stage. Betty has no alibi. She was home here…alone."

"Pfft." Charlotte swished her hand, dismissing his words. "So was probably half of Ashton Point. And let me point out it would be more damning if her fingerprints *hadn't* been found on the crutch, wouldn't you agree, Detective Anderson?"

His jaw dropped and a sliver of hope bloomed in her chest. All those years of watching real-life crime shows was paying off. "Surely whoever assaulted this man would've wanted to cover their tracks by wiping their prints off and, at the same time leaving my grandma's." She was on a roll. "For that matter, how do you know he was attacked with the elbow crutch? And why leave it there, why not take it with them and dispose of it?"

Anger burned bright in his eyes and his lips pursed together in a thin line. "All I can say at this point is it has been confirmed the crutch found beside Mr Pantell is the assault weapon. As for your other points, I'll take them into consideration."

Betty cleared her throat and placed a hand on Charlotte's forearm. "Detective Anderson, it appears you have what they call on television circumstantial evidence. I will not have my name associated with such a ghastly act. Rest assured, I will not be leaving town until the real assailant is safely behind bars."

Charlotte pulled Betty into her side and held her tight. "That goes for me too."

Anderson sighed, a note of resignation filled the air. "Fine, but stay where I can reach you. I *will* have further questions."

Charlotte squeezed Betty once more then followed him out, locking the door behind him. She leant her head against the door and squeezed her eyes shut.

So much for a quiet weekend with Grandma.

Chapter Three

BETTY POURED HER second cup of Earl Grey tea for the morning and stifled another yawn. Sleep hadn't come easy. Detective Anderson's accusation sat heavy on her heart, only beaten by the continual hammering of the storm against the roof. She'd finally drifted off around one-thirty, after the two Panadol she took kicked in and the fuzziness clouding her mind dissipated. Betty turned at the muffled scuffing of slippers coming down the hallway.

"Morning. Grandma, you should've woken me up earlier," Charlotte said. She flopped down into a kitchen chair, tightening her hot pink fluffy robe round her waist, her bright red wavy locks gathered on top of her head in a messy ponytail.

"Good morning, love. Why on earth would I wake you? You need your sleep, sweetheart." Betty smiled. Charlotte had the ruffled sleep look down pat. "Would you like tea or coffee?"

"Coffee thanks. My usual drug of addiction." Charlotte turned and glanced out the kitchen window. "I can't believe it's still raining."

Betty placed a steaming cup of freshly brewed coffee in front of Charlotte and watched her eyes widen as she inhaled the aroma. "Yes, I knew we were in for a light shower but there was no storm predicted. That will teach me to trust the weather forecast."

Charlotte sipped her coffee, her eyelids closing while she savoured the addictive liquid. She paused and looked Betty square in the eyes. "Okay Grandma, sit and tell me all about this Pantell guy, the one who was attacked, your foot and everything you did in the last twenty-four hours. And don't leave a single detail out."

Betty opened her mouth in protest, but her words would fall on deaf ears. Of her three granddaughters, Charlotte followed in her footsteps in every way from determination to her exceptional cooking skills. "It all started at the meeting in the town hall yesterday morning."

Betty watched a myriad of expressions cross Charlotte's face as she relayed the previous day's events in detail. "And then you turned up. Which, although a nice surprise, is a somewhat unexpected one." The colour drained from Charlotte's face and the spark in her eyes diminished as though someone extinguished the light inside her. Betty reached for Charlotte's hand and cupped it tightly. "What happened darling girl? Why the sudden appearance?"

Charlotte paused, biting her lower lip. "It's Gary."

"That nice young man you've been dating?" Betty asked.

Charlotte's jaw dropped and anger flared in her eyes. "Nice? Nice. Ha. That *nice* young man is a two-timing married jerk."

Betty frowned. "Oh dear."

"Yeah, oh dear is right. I found out yesterday when he turned up with his *wife* to pick up their two-year anniversary cake. All I could think about was getting away from Sydney as fast as I could. I always feel better when I'm here with you. It's just under three hours to drive. Took me no time at all." Charlotte shook her head and drained the last of her coffee. "Let's forget about Gary. We have more important things to do like clearing your name and finding out who wanted to silence Derek Pantell. Permanently."

* * *

Charlotte paced the small kitchen, energy flaring in her belly. "What time was the attack again?"

"Detective Anderson said between one and one-thirty yesterday afternoon. I got home about twelve forty-five and Laurel rang at two o'clock. I was home here cleaning with no alibi at the time of the attack," Betty said, her words deflated.

"Right and your appointment was at midday with Dr Harrison?" Charlotte asked, confirming in her mind once more. "That's a tight window, but at this stage we don't have enough information. We don't even know where the attack happened and if they found him in the same location as the attack took place. Detective Anderson wasn't very forthcoming with information, was he?"

Betty chimed in. "No. Most of the people in the meeting yesterday wanted to throttle the man. The town is against the development, full stop. Maybe some of them conspired together to take out the one man dead set on destroying our town." Uncertainty hung in the air like a bad smell.

Betty's growing silence clawed at Charlotte's heart. Longing to comfort her, Charlotte knelt beside Betty and gathered her warm hands. "It will all work out in the end. I'm going to do everything in my power to help you and if all else fails, we'll call in reinforcements from the city."

Betty's eyes widened, and she shook her head. "No, love. I don't want your parents bothered with this."

Charlotte pulled back, a heaviness filling her chest. "But—"

"No, they have enough to worry about with their busy lives. You and I possess enough smarts between us to wipe the floor with that pompous detective. Promise me, Charlotte Amber McCorrson."

Charlotte cringed. Grandma only used her full name when she wanted to drive her point home. "Okay, I promise, but I draw the line when it comes to our safety. If you or I are in danger, then all bets are off. Do I make myself clear?"

"That's fair, I suppose," Betty said, cupping Charlotte's cheek in her palm. "Between you and me, I think we've got this in the bag."

Adrenaline burned through her system at the challenge. "You're right, but the first thing we need is information and like any small town there's one place where they run it on tap." She stood and pulled her hair from the ponytail examining the ends. "I think it's time I made an impromptu visit to the Classic Curl."

Betty bolted from her seat. "Of course. If there's information to be learned, you can be sure the girls at the Classic Curl hairdressing salon will know. And while you're there, I think I'll take a visit to the nursing home. Bob might not be there any longer, but I still have friends on the inside."

"What do you say we meet back here at midday and compare notes?"

"Sounds like a plan, Dick Tracy," Betty said in a mysterious gruff voice giving Charlotte a wink. "Make sure you rug up in this weather, we can't exactly solve a crime if we both end up in hospital with pneumonia."

Both ladies burst out laughing, filling Charlotte's chest with warmth.

* * *

The bitter wind whistled in Charlotte's ears sending shivers barrelling up her spine as she rushed toward the entrance of the Classic Curl. Her tied up hair now an impromptu mess resembling a tangled fishing net. "This weather is crazy," she muttered, straining to close the door against the force of the howling wind. A resounding bang as it slammed shut reverberated through the small salon causing Charlotte to jump. She turned receiving an onslaught of frowns and eyebrow raises from customers. She smiled sheepishly and shrugged. "Sorry, that was totally the wind's fault."

A petite woman with long blond hair down to her waist rushed over and grabbed Charlotte's wet coat. Her glittery gold name badge read *Shelly*. "Are you all right? This weather is causing a right shemozzle almost everywhere in town." She hung the coat on the rack and headed back to the counter popping a pair of Cath Kidston designer specs on the end of her nose. "Do you have an appointment?"

"Um no. I was hoping you could squeeze me in for a wash and trim," Charlotte said, behind her *'please feel sorry for me,'* puppy dog eyes. "I'm Charlotte McCorrson, Betty Brookson's granddaughter."

Shelly's eyes widened. "Of course. Didn't I see you and your family a few weeks back? At O' Shay's Restaurant at the Country Club with Betty?"

Charlotte nodded, the memory of the family get-together held fond memories in her heart. "We all came up from Sydney for Grandma's birthday. Me, mum and dad, and my sisters, Clair and Cassidy."

"Oh, how lovely." She paused. "To have family who care about you that much they'd travel up to visit on your birthday."

Shelly's sarcastic tone was not lost on Charlotte.

"Okay let's see here," Shelly said, scanning the appointment book. "You're in luck, Stefanie's ten-thirty has moved to Monday so she can do you in about ten minutes."

Triumph warmed her insides. "Perfect."

Thirty minutes later, she sat in a black plastic gown and washed hair in the hands of the salon owner, Stefanie. Charlotte's insides churned and her mind ticked over with a million and one questions.

Questions without answers served no purpose.

She glanced at Stefanie in the mirror. "I'm so grateful you could fit me in on such short notice. I mean with all the drama of the last twenty-four hours and all. It must have been a total shock."

Stefanie's scissors snipped continually. "Shock?"

"You know…the brutal assault," Charlotte whispered, planting the bait. "I was truly mortified when I heard about what that poor man suffered. To think it happened in my grandma's hometown."

"I know. First the kerfuffle at the town meeting yesterday. I thought we were going to have a riot on our hands." Stefanie's paused, and she glanced left then right checking the coast was clear. A sly grin turning the corner of her lips up. She leant in closer and whispered, "I'm not usually one to gossip, but apparently someone took to him with something heavy and battered his head in."

Charlotte's stomach knotted.

Yeah, with grandma's elbow crutch.

"Did you hear they found him in the pool at the nursing home?"

Charlotte held her breath, Stefanie's words adding another nail in grandma's case. Her hands twisting together in her lap, she asked. "Even though his head was bashed in?"

She nodded. "I also heard from Joe's wife who found out from Olivia who works at Ashton Point Library that Kurtis from AP Tyres had a huge public row with the man outside after the meeting. A lot of town folk were pretty riled up and none too shy in telling him what they thought."

Charlotte fought the adrenaline coursing through her veins. Another possible suspect. She wanted to jump up and fist pump the air. "Gosh, poor man, he's lucky he didn't drown?"

The words flowed from her lips like liquid gold. "There was blood smeared everywhere, all over the pool area."

Charlotte gasped in mock horror while her insides were doing hi-fives.

Stefanie continued, barely taking a breath. "That's what I can't work out."

"What?" Charlotte hung off her every word.

"If the blow to his head did the damage, why did they find him in the water?" Stefanie asked.

Why indeed?

"Maybe they figured the pool would finish him off. You know, make it look like drowning. I bet they were praying no one would find the body." Stefanie held up a hand mirror behind Charlotte's head and smiled. "What do you think?"

She swivelled her head from side to side admiring Stefanie's handiwork. "I love it. Thank you."

A deafening clap of thunder cracked through the sky shaking the entire salon. Shelly's hands shot to her ears. "Holy cow, that was close."

"I think that's my cue to leave. I'm so glad I got a park right out front of the salon," Charlotte said, as she glanced toward the front door. "I'd like to get back home before it gets any worse. Thanks for squeezing me in."

"No problem," Stefanie said, picking up the broom. "Head down to the counter and Shelly will fix your payment."

Charlotte nodded and busied herself pulling several notes out of her purse as she approached the counter. The conversation caught her attention and her pulse raced into overdrive. She slowed her movements, soaking up every tad bit of gossip.

"Oh my gosh, Beverly, what you nurses do is amazing. I can't believe you were so close to where that poor man was attacked. You could have been next," Shelly said, her voice raked with concern.

Charlotte glanced sideways at the woman in question. Her wet shoulder length mousy brown hair clung to her damp skin and her hazel eyes fixated on Shelly. With a single swipe of her wrist, she flung her hair over her shoulder, water droplets cascading onto the counter. "It was a total shock. I mean a man attacked in our perfect little nursing home. I couldn't believe it when I heard about it."

Hope lightened Charlotte's heart. Beverly could hold the answers. "I didn't mean to eavesdrop, but did I hear right? You work at the nursing home?"

Beverly turned and glared, annoyance creasing her brow. "Yes, you heard correct." A flip of her head dismissed Charlotte as if she were invisible.

No one dismisses me, thank you very much.

Her stomach muscles coiled tight. But she let a giggle escape her lips. "Oh my gosh, please excuse my rudeness, I'm Charlotte McCorrson, Betty Brookson's granddaughter. Grandma was saying she left the nursing home not long before it happened."

The lines in Beverly's forehead eased and a brief smile crossed her lips. "Nice to meet you. She was very lucky then."

"Did Detective Anderson say what happened?" Shelley took the words right out of Charlotte's mouth.

Beverly shook her head. "No."

"So, you don't know what happened?" Charlotte asked.

Beverly's frown returned. "No. But then again, after the meeting yesterday I expect most of Ashton

Point would want to see him gone, but never like that."

Questions fired hot from Charlotte's lips. "Were you at the meeting?"

"Yes, of course."

"And did you speak up?"

Beverly shrugged and shook her head. "I was going to. He left before I had the chance. But why anyone would want to drown someone, I'll never know."

Charlotte pulled back, her gaze drilling Beverly like a red-hot poker. "Drown? On the town gossip vine they said he was bludgeoned."

Beverly continued. "Detective Anderson didn't say, but I assumed because they found him face down in the hydro pool, he drowned. But I guess I could be wrong."

"Poor man, and it happened so close to you. Where you scared?" Charlotte asked. "I know I would have freaked out."

"No. I wasn't there," Beverly said. Her hand clutched her neck, and a sigh eased from her lips. Her gaze moved from Charlotte to Shelley and back again, like watching a tennis match. "My shift finished at midday and I was home by twelve-thirty snuggled up on my couch with a rug and a coffee ready to watch Sweet Hearts at one. I hadn't heard about the incident until Detective Anderson came to my house yesterday afternoon to ask me a few routine questions. I was just as shocked as anyone."

Charlotte watched Shelly's eyes sparkle as she absorbed up every word like a sponge. "To think such an awful act of violence could tarnish our beautiful little town. I hope they catch the culprit before anyone else gets hurt."

"Me too." She handed over her money, her car keys jingling from her ring finger. "I best be off before this storm really takes hold. Thanks again for squeezing me in, Shelly."

Shelly smiled. "No problem."

Charlotte left and her heart sank with each step.

A dead end.

Chapter Four

"FOR GOODNESS SAKE, Clair, take a breath and listen for two seconds." Charlotte huffed and rolled her eyes. "I'm fine. Honestly." She squished the phone handset between her shoulder and ear and stretched to the fridge for milk. Why grandma still had an old corded landline, she'd never know.

"I've a good mind to track down that no good cheat and give him a piece of my mind," Clair barked.

Charlotte smiled and a warm fuzziness filled her heart. "You know I love you, but I don't need my big sister fighting my battles for me. Anyway, he's not worth it."

I've got bigger problems than my cheating married ex-boyfriend.

"How's Grandma," Clair asked. "Not getting into mischief I hope."

Charlotte's stomach dropped and she swallowed the lump in her throat. Remembering her promise, she chose her words carefully. "Um, she's good. Keeping busy as usual. You know grandma."

Silence on the end of the line paused Charlotte's train of thought. "Clair…Clair, are you there?" Charlotte looked at the handset, her lips pinched together. "Great, the phone's dead."

Replacing the handset in its cradle, she reached for her mobile.

Thank you for caring, but I'm fine. Bad storm here, I'll call you when it passes.

She sent the text to Claire. "Damn it, reception's gone." She pulled the curtain back and a shudder goose bumped her skin sending shivers racing up her arms. Rain pelted the window, and the wind danced a raging gale through the trees. The storm had reared its ugly head again, playing havoc with the phone lines.

What next?

"Candles." She rummaged around in the kitchen draws praying grandma was still safe at the nursing home. "She must have candles here somewhere."

Third drawer down she struck gold and held up a bag of candles and matches. "Now we're in business. All set if the power goes out."

A sharp click. The front door? Her breath in her throat, she eased around the kitchen doorway. "Grandma?"

Betty's voice floated from the front of the house. "Yes, love, it's me or what's left of me."

A vice grip tightened around Charlotte's chest.

What's that supposed to mean?

Betty turned the corner and stood still, her jaw clenched, and her lips pursed. Drenched from head to toe, her beautiful silver-streaked hair hanging bedraggled around her wet face. Her appearance resembled a puddle-drenched doll. Charlotte's hand flew to her mouth to muffle an escaping giggle.

Betty flopped her bag onto the kitchen bench and her cheeks reddened. "That will be enough out of you, young lady. I know I look a sight, but what can you expect when it's raining buckets out there."

"I'm sorry, it's just you look so…so…wet." Charlotte giggled like a cheeky school girl. "Why don't you go take a shower and warm up, I'll prepare lunch and then we can chat?"

"Does lunch come with a peppermint tea?" Betty pouted, folding her arms across her chest.

Charlotte gasped in mock horror. "Is there any other?"

Betty relaxed, and a smile twitched her lips. "Okay, you're forgiven. I'll be back once I feel half-human again."

"No rush," Charlotte called after her.

* * *

"Ah, that's better," Betty muttered. She wrapped her cardigan tight around her chest and headed down the hallway. The scent of peppermint drifted from the kitchen and she sucked in a deep mouthful. As she turned the corner, her gaze landed on the table set with her favourite white embroidered linen tablecloth. A warm glow filled her chest as she watched Charlotte put the finishing touches on their lunch.

Of her three granddaughters, Charlotte was the most like her. Strong willed and determined with the biggest heart and the capacity to love unconditionally.

And an award-winning cook. Longing burrowed itself deep in her heart. Since Bob passed away, Edith and Mark had been on about her moving to Sydney with them. As much as she loved her family, moving in with her daughter and son-in-law was not the way she wanted to live out the rest of her life. A burden to her family, she was not. How could she leave her beloved Ashton Point? Bob may not be here, but her heart and soul was very much alive and embedded within the small-town community.

"Grandma, I didn't see you there," Charlotte said with a smile looking up from the table. "Come and eat."

"Thank you, my girl." Taking her place opposite Charlotte, she glanced toward the window. "Thank goodness the storm's let up."

"Yeah, the phone lines are still down though."

Betty filled her plate with salad and leftover lasagne, the whole time ignoring the grumble roaring from her belly. "Tell me what you found out at the Classic Curl this morning."

Charlotte took a bite and shuffled forward on her chair, then she paused to eat.

"Well come on, don't keep me in suspense." Charlotte's sapphire blue eyes sparkled with excitement and a bubble of anticipation worked its way up Betty's chest.

Charlotte swallowed the last of her mouthful and laughed. "Don't they say patience is a virtue?"

"Pfft," Betty hissed, swishing her hand in the air as if swatting flies. "You know patience has never been my friend. Now spill."

"Well, apart from getting a fantastic wash and trim, my visit was more interesting than I expected. Once I got Stefanie talking, there was no stopping her and believe you me, she had a lot to say. It was like trying to stop mum describing her latest interior design project."

I know exactly what you mean.

Betty's chest clenched, and a pang gripped her heart. It was times like these she missed the most. Family meal time.

"Stefanie was quick to point out his head was beaten in with something heavy."

Betty harrumphed. "That much we knew."

Charlotte continued. "But what intrigued me was the bit about Kurtis from AP Tyres. Apparently, he had a very public row with the man outside the town hall after the meeting yesterday. Stefanie thought there would be a riot."

Betty gasped and her jaw dropped. "No."

Charlotte nodded, gulping half a glass of soft drink. "Yep, but it doesn't stop there. Stefanie said they found the poor man in the pool at the nursing home. The question is, why put him in the pool if he was beaten to within an inch of his life?"

A niggle in the base of Betty's neck stopped her mid-thought. Her gut knotted. Her mind ran through her conversation with Hattie from the nursing home. Something didn't feel right.

What am I missing?

Clarity shot through like a torpedo. She snapped her fingers and looked straight at Charlotte's animated eyes. "The pool."

"Yeah, they found him in the pool, but—"

Betty cut Charlotte's words short. "But the pool has been closed. Hattie said it had some sort of bacterial infection and it wasn't safe for patients to use *and* they'd kept it locked for the past week."

"Then how does a dead body end up behind locked doors?" Charlotte asked.

Betty sighed, rubbing her temple. "That's the million-dollar question, isn't it? You did good, love."

"Oh, I'm not finished," Charlotte said, bounding with energy. "As I was leaving, I happened to run into Beverly."

Betty's brow creased. "Beverly Wattson, the nurse?"

Charlotte nodded. "Yep. A bit stuck up if you ask me, but then she found out I was your granddaughter and she softened. Anyway, her shift finished at midday."

Midday?

Charlotte stood and began clearing the table. "She found out about the assault when Detective Anderson called by her house yesterday afternoon to ask some routine questions. Luckily, she was home, so she missed the whole debacle."

"What time did she get home?" Betty pried.

"Twelve-thirty."

Twelve-thirty? No, that can't be right.

A shiver raced up Betty's spine. "How can that be?"

Charlotte turned, a frown crinkling her forehead. "What do you mean?"

"I saw her car, it was still outside the nursing home when I left. You can't miss it, it's a bright canary yellow Swift. How can she be in two places at once? I suppose she could have gotten a lift home." Betty's stomach did crazy somersaults and not the gold medal ones, the complete opposite.

Charlotte shrugged and continued clearing the table. "Maybe she did. Either way, she managed to get home to watch her favourite show Sweet Hearts at one. Can't say I've seen it myself. Who has time to watch daytime soaps? Not me."

Alarm skyrocketed Betty's pulse.

Charlotte's eyes widened. "Grandma, are you all right? You look like you've seen a ghost. You're almost as white as the tablecloth."

"I wish I'd seen a ghost," she said, her chest knotting as her thoughts strung together. "Beverly got it wrong. Sweet Hearts start at two, not one. I should know, I watch it religiously. I may be old, but I know good eye candy when I see it. She lied and, if she lied about the show time maybe she lied about leaving the nursing home when she did. Maybe the reason I saw her car was because she was still there."

Charlotte eased herself into the chair beside Betty. "There was one other thing she mentioned at the salon today and I brushed it aside, but now it could be important."

"What is it?" Betty asked, squeezing Charlotte's hand. A silent source of support.

"She said the body was found face down in the pool. How would she know unless Detective Anderson told her or, *she* left the body that way after bashing his skull in?"

Chapter Five

AN EERIE SILENCE descended upon the kitchen interrupted only by the howling wind scraping the tree branches along the side of the gutter. "Or we could be over thinking this way too much," Betty said, patting Charlotte's hand. "No use jumping to conclusions."

Charlotte shot up from the chair. "Today in the salon I could have chatted to the woman responsible for putting Mr Pantell in a coma. Either way, I think we should pass this information onto Detective Anderson sooner rather than later." Charlotte snatched the landline handset and listened. A frown crossed her expression. A picture of disappointment.

"What's wrong?" Betty asked.

Returning the handset, she picked up her mobile. Her eyes widened. "Bingo. Receptions back." A cacophony of high-pitched beeps echoed like discorded music as message after message came through.

"What on earth is that noise?"

Charlotte moved her fingers across the keypad, silencing the racket. "Just messages. I'll check them later. Have you got Detective Anderson's number, Grandma?"

"Of course," Betty nodded and pointed to the Teledex on the kitchen counter beside the pantry. "I make a point of saving all the important numbers." Betty's stomach clenched as Charlotte dialled.

"Detective Anderson, this is Charlotte McCorrson, Betty Brookson's granddaughter," she said with a slight quiver in her voice. "Yes, I'm fine and so is grandma. Detective, I'll come straight to the point. I was wondering if you told anyone how Mr Pantell's body was found in the pool?"

Charlotte bit her lip while she listened. "Um, it might have something to do with the attack, I'm not sure. Is it public knowledge how the body was found? Face up or face down?" She asked once more.

Betty watched the blood drain from Charlotte's face. "What is it? What did he say?" Betty whispered, her impatience clawing at her from the inside out.

Charlotte held her finger up and mouthed, "one sec."

"Then yes, we have some significant information for you. I'm sure it will help catch the attacker. In fact, I'm certain of it."

"At home, but we—" Charlotte gasped, her voice dropped mid-sentence.

"What's wrong?" Betty asked, her throat tightened like a vice.

Tutting, Charlotte said, "Great. This just isn't our day. Your phone line is dead and mine just dropped out. We'll be lucky if we *can* get the information to Detective Anderson."

"What did he say?" Betty asked, irritation twisting her insides.

"We were right. They haven't released any details, which means Beverly had to be there to know how the body was found. I'm not saying she attacked him, but she must have been in the pool area with the body to know he was face down in the pool."

Charlotte's concern mirrored Betty's own. "I'll tell you what. I was heading over to Laurel's after lunch to give her some of my special herbal remedy to settle her nasty cough, I'll call into the police station on the way and see Detective Anderson?"

"Grandma, surely you're not going out in this weather again?" Charlotte said, her eyes wide in disbelief.

"Of course," she said, with a curt laugh. "It's only rain and wind. It's not the first storm to hit Ashton Point and it won't be the last. Life goes on."

Charlotte's lips thinned and she folded her arms across her chest. "Fine, then I'm going with you."

Betty's mouth opened into a round 'O', but Charlotte held her finger up before she could object.

"*And* I'm not taking no for an answer." Charlotte stood her ground, her stern gaze fastening Betty to the chair like glue. "So, what's it going to be? We do this together or I get a pack of cards out and I whip your butt in gin rummy just like I did the last time I was here."

Warmth bloomed in Betty's heart. Charlotte's sapphire blue eyes shimmered against the warm fluorescent light while her beautiful wavy red locks hovered around her shoulders. She had a soft spot for her middle granddaughter. Kindred spirit all the way.

Betty rose from her chair and her lips curved upward. She whispered, "I'll let you in on a little secret." Charlotte's brow furrowed. "I let you win."

Charlotte huffed. "You did not. I beat you fair and square. In fact, I'll prove it. I challenge you to a rematch. When we get back from visiting Detective Anderson and Laurel, you and I are sitting down and playing, and I'll show you just how much you let me win. What do you say?"

The smugness branded across Charlotte's face spiked the competitor lurking deep inside Betty. "You're on. Let's do this."

Charlotte giggled and threw her arms around Betty, squeezing the life out of her. "I love you so much, Grandma. You're the best."

"Glad you think so, love. I love you too. Now, let's be on our way."

"I'll drive," Charlotte said, grabbing her bag and keys off the kitchen bench.

* * *

Charlotte slowed to ten kilometres under the speed limit, her knuckles whitening under her grip on the steering wheel. Rain pelted down forming a scattered symphony against the windscreen. Her nerves already on edge intensified by the water covered road. "Here I was thinking the storm had let up. How can there be virtually no rain fifteen minutes ago and now, it's a torrential downpour?"

"That's Mother Nature for you," Betty said.

Another rapid concession of high-pitched beeps from her handbag battled the constant drone of the rain. "Phone reception's back again. Probably my messages from Clair or Detective Anderson."

Betty asked, "Clair?"

Charlotte nodded and turned down toward St. Edwards point. The road sparse of its normal Saturday afternoon traffic.

Looks like grandma and I are the only ones brave enough to tackle the roads.

Charlotte continued. "Clair rung on your phone after I got in from the salon and we were cut off when the line went dead. I guess she had more to say."

"Would you like me to check them for you?" Betty asked, pausing a moment. "Although if it's private, I can leave it for you to check while I'm in with Laurel."

Private? Hardly. She shook her head. "No, it's fine. You'll find it in the inside pocket. It's not like you don't know what happened with Gary."

The tension eased from Charlotte's chest as the rain slowed to a light shower. Betty hummed her favourite Doris Day tune as she searched her bag. Charlotte made a silent promise to herself to spend more time with her grandma in future, after all, she wouldn't be around forever.

Charlotte chanced a quick sideways glance and chuckled at the sight before her. A petulant frown drew Betty's brows together and her lips pursed in determination as she fiddled with the buttons on Charlotte's phone.

The sudden shriek of Betty's voice rung out like death, sending terror racing through her body. "Everything okay there?" Charlotte asked. She knew Betty had no idea how to work her touch screen mobile.

"Charlotte look out," Betty screamed. The phone slipped from her grasp and her hand flew to the dashboard. With her other hand, Betty pointed to the car barrelling toward them on a collision course.

Charlotte's pulse skyrocketed and heart jumped into her throat. "What the hell?" she said, swerving to avoid the impact, her car spinning out of control on the wet road.

Oh my God, we're gonna die.

The wheels skidded on the wet road. Panic screamed through her veins as she worked to control the car. Fear pulverised her ribcage. She yelled, "Hold on." Then threw her left arm across Betty's chest thrusting her back in the seat a split second before the car veered off the road and into the side ditch crashing into a half-submerged old tree stump.

Pain throbbed in Charlotte's temple. Her heavy eyelids fluttered open and her gaze blurred against a heavy fog drowning her senses. "What…happp…"

A scratchy voice beside her sent her weak with relief. "You…you saved us."

"Oh my God, Grandma are you all right?" she asked. Ignoring her own pain, she fussed over the woman who meant the world to her. Her words rushed out while her anxieties shot through the roof like an out-of-control rocket ship. "Talk to me, is anything broken? Are you okay? Where does it hurt?"

"Yes, love. A little shaken and they'll be a few bruises, but on the whole, I think I'm fine." Betty winced as she reached to undo her seat belt. "It was no accident, that car deliberately ran us off the road."

"No kidding."

Betty added. "And if I'm not mistaken, it was a yellow Swift."

Fear gripped every muscle in Charlotte's body.

Holy cow, it was Beverly. She ran us off the road.

"The phone, Grandma. Where's my phone?" Charlotte asked, her hands shaking.

Betty cast her eyes downward. "The floor. I dropped it when I saw the blinding car lights in our path."

Adrenaline coursed through her like lightening. She released her seatbelt and dived toward Betty's feet, both hands combing the floor for the missing object. Triumph exploded as she grabbed the phone as though it were gold.

Please have reception, please have reception.

"Sweetheart? We need to get out of here…now. Look." Charlotte baulked at the fear in Betty's tone.

Her head whipped to the right following Betty's gaze. Terror nauseated her insides. Headlights were heading straight for them. "Oh God, she's coming back. Get out, Grandma. Quick, into the bush and find a hiding place. I know you're hurt, but it's going to be a damn sight worse if she finds us."

Within minutes they'd found a small wall of shrubs tall enough to hide from peering eyes. Her body shivered as cool rain showered down, but she didn't budge. "Be quiet and don't move," Charlotte said. Her shaky fingers hit the re-dial button. "Detective Anderson?" she whispered. "Please help us. It's Beverly Wattson, she's the one who attacked Mr Pantell, and she just ran my car off the road."

"What the hell… Are you okay? Is Betty with you?" he blurted.

Charlotte heaved air into her lungs. She ran her hand though her wet hair scrapping back the strands glued to her cheeks. "Yes, we're okay but she's coming back."

"What…Beverly Wattson? How do you know?" he asked.

Adrenaline rushed through her body as Beverly pulled to a stop. "Yes, Beverly Wattson. I'll explain everything when you get here. We're hiding in the bushes about a kilometre past St. Edward's point turnoff by the old rusted car wreck on the way into town. Hurry." The familiar silence of the deadline bit at Charlotte and her heart ran its own marathon inside her chest.

Chapter Six

"OH, COME NOW, Charlotte? You don't really think you can hide from me, do you?" Beverly called from the side of the road.

The disturbing voice froze Betty's blood. Contempt lacing her words, she sensed it was only a matter of time before she discovered their hiding place.

"I knew I'd made a blunder today at the salon. I screwed up, but I got so flustered with all the nosy questions. You and I both know the only way I knew the body was found face down in the pool was if I'd been there. I've already got blood on my hands, what's one or two more? You couldn't leave well enough alone, could you?"

Betty held her breath and squeezed Charlotte's hand. Charlotte mouthed the words, 'don't move', but she needn't bother. Panic seized her body and she couldn't get up if she tried.

"Didn't they tell you driving in this weather can be dangerous…very dangerous. Such a shame you lost control of your car," Beverly said. "Injuries happen from car accidents, deadly injuries."

Betty peered through a gap in the bushes and zeroed in on the woman standing beside Charlotte's car. Her foreboding stance screamed danger. She held a long baseball bat-like object in her hand. There was no question in Betty's mind, she was there to wreak havoc.

Betty saw Charlotte slowly bend down and pick up a rock the size of her hand and pitched it as far as she could to the left. Beverly jumped and her head whipped around toward the loud rustle where it landed, her bat up poised ready to strike.

"This *is* going to end today. One way or another."

Charlotte fiddled with her phone keypad and then flipped it toward Betty, the screen barely alight with the word 'record' and her finger to her lips in a shushing action. The bush around them closed in on her, suffocating every breath in her body.

Betty wanted to scream, *No! Don't do it, don't bait her.*

"If it's going to end, Beverly, the least you could do is tell me why that man deserved the beating you gave him," Charlotte called.

Betty admired the calmness Charlotte's voice projected, but her shaking hands told another story. She almost shook the phone from her grip.

"He could have died."

The vehemence in Beverly's tone intensified. "He *was* supposed to die. How the hell he survived I'll never know."

Betty peered through the bushes again. Her insides so nauseated cramps gripped her as though King Kong trapped her in his gigantic hand and squeezed.

"Why? Why do it?" Charlotte asked.

"Like you'd understand," Beverly bit back as she slowly began edging her way toward the front of Charlotte's car. "You can't tell me you wouldn't do anything for your family, especially for Betty."

Charlotte paled and our eyes locked together. Hers mirrored the fear raking through my body.

Detective Anderson, where are you?

Charlotte persisted. "Maybe you're right, but I don't understand?"

"Because my grandmother was next," Beverly roared between heaving breaths. "She was next on the list for a bed in the nursing home. I couldn't stand to keep her in that awful disgusting home she's currently in any longer. I did everything right. Doctor Harrison asked me to return Betty's crutches to the pharmacy, and I was on my way when his nasal voice assaulted my eardrums. He was there…at the nursing home. He was going to flatten the place by the end of the week. Then what was I supposed to do? That man just wouldn't listen. I asked politely, I even begged, and you know what he said?"

"What?"

"He said my grandmother wasn't his problem. The land was worth more to him as apartments than my grandmother's life would ever be worth," Beverly said between sobs. "He didn't care about anyone but himself. I was furious. I raised the crutch and hit him. Hard. Again and again and again."

A blanket shiver covered Betty's body. The cold sinister tone of the woman's voice sent her blood cold.

"Now stop avoiding the inevitable, Charlotte." Beverly slowly raised the bat above her head. "Make it easy for both of us and come out before I come in there and make what I did to Mr Pantell look like—"

A sharp cocking of a gun froze her mid-sentence. "I don't think so." Detective Anderson stood on the other side of the road, his gun pin-pointed at Beverly. "Just in case you missed it, that noise was the bullet locking into the chamber of my gun pointed at you. It's your call what happens from here, Beverly."

She paused, the bat tumbled from her hands crashing on the bitumen and she raised them above her head in surrender.

Betty sucked in a lungful of air into her starved lungs. "Charlotte?"

"Oh Grandma, it's over," she said as she dropped into Betty's open arms. She held on tight and soaked up the sweet scent of her brave granddaughter. Charlotte's rapid heartbeat thumped against her chest. A joyful reminder of how close she came to losing such a dear soul.

Anderson's gruff voice called, "Great job ladies. Thanks for keeping her talking. I've got all the evidence I need to ensure Beverly here, goes away for a long time. Are you okay? Is anyone hurt?"

Charlotte pulled back and wiped fresh tears with the back of her palm. "Yes, Detective, we are fine. A little banged up but nothing a little rest and a lot of peppermint tea won't fix."

* * *

"Grandma, what did the doctor say?" Charlotte snapped as she entered the kitchen, rushing to grab the oversize cardboard box from Betty's hands. "Rest for at least a week. It's only been five days."

Betty sighed and pulled Charlotte into a hug. "Oh love, you're such a worrywart. The doctor said take it easy and only do activities not causing me pain or aggravating my injuries." Betty pulled back. "Carrying a box of baking trays in from the garage hardly constitutes a strenuous activity."

Charlotte pouted. "Regardless, I want you taking it easy until at least Sunday, got it?" Betty shot her hands up in surrender. "Now make yourself comfortable, peppermint tea coming right up."

"You don't have to tell me twice." Betty eased into the closest chair. She blinked back tears at the sight of Charlotte's bag by the door. Clearing her throat, she said, "I never really got a chance to thank you for the way you handled the situation with your mother. I could have sworn she'd shoot up here once she found out what happened."

Charlotte shrugged dismissively, placing two steaming cups of tea on the table. "Mum's all right, you just need to know the best way to handle her. Besides, I was here mending my broken heart, and she trusts me, and she trusts you."

Betty's brows raised. "You're having tea?"

"After the excitement of the weekend I figured I should cut the caffeine." Charlotte puckered her lips to blow the rising steam. "Now Beverly is behind bars and my recording safely in the hands of the police, I guess it's a waiting game to see what Pantell will do now he's out of a coma."

The shrill landline rung out and startled Charlotte into spilling her tea. "Ouch," she said, shaking her hand.

"Careful sweetheart." Betty grabbed the phone, tossing a hand towel toward Charlotte. "Hello."

Laurel's velvety voice caressed Betty's ear. "Betty, I can't believe it. Have you heard?"

"Heard what?" she asked.

"Pantell withdrew the contract on the nursing home this morning." Her voice laced with excitement. "As soon as he can, he's leaving town, said the city was much safer."

"Are you sure?" Betty's knees weakened as elation bubbled in her belly.

"Positive. Isn't it wonderful?"

"It certainly is, Laurel. Although a shame it had to happen this way, but all the same I'm glad the nursing home is staying." Charlotte's forehead crinkled as she glanced at Betty. "Laurel, can I call you back in a little while?"

"Of course."

"Thanks again for the great news," Betty said, ending the call.

Charlotte swivelled around in her chair. "What's going on?"

"Pantell withdrew the contract on the nursing home and is leaving Ashton Point." The words rolled off her tongue and settled in the air.

Charlotte squealed and shot off her chair like a firecracker. "Woohoo. That's the best news I've heard since…since Detective Anderson's voice last Saturday."

"You know Charlotte, small town life suits you," Betty said as she gave her girl a hug. A slice of her heart wilted knowing when Charlotte left, she would most probably have to wait until Christmas to see her again. See all her beautiful granddaughters again. She smiled and put on a brave face. "I haven't seen you this relaxed since you arrived."

"I haven't been this relaxed in a long time." Charlotte threw her arms around Betty and squeezed so tight her chest barely sucked in air. "Thank you for letting me mend my broken heart here, Grandma. I need to go back to Sydney and deal with the fallout. But you know you only have to call, and I'll be here in a jiffy as will Clair and Cassidy."

"I know."

Charlotte continued. "You are right about one thing."

"What's that dear?"

"Ashton Point brings out the best in people. Leaving Saturday's nightmare out of it, being here with you this past week has reminded me family means everything. And not just blood relatives. Family are the people you love, those around you who you love. Ashton Point is busting with love."

"Here, here!" Betty said, smiling against Charlotte's cheek.

Charlotte's eyes sparkled like polished sapphires. "You never know I might be back sooner than you think."

"The door will always be open for you, my dear. After all, we're family."

The End

Thank you for reading **Cupcakes and Conspiracy.** If you enjoyed this story, I would really appreciate it if you would consider leaving a review of this book, no matter how short, at the retailer site where you bought your copy or on sites like Amazon and Goodreads.

YOU are the key to this book's success and the success of **The Cupcake Capers Culinary Cozy Mystery Series.**

I read every review and they really do make a huge difference.

Continue reading The Cupcake Capers Series

Visit my website below to continue reading the series through your favourite ebook retailer.

https://www.pollyholmesmysteries.com/the-cupcake-capers

To order print books in The Cupcake Capers series, please email Gumnut Press on the email below to place your order.

info@gumnutpres.com

Stay in the Loop

Love new releases, free books, and a little behind-the-scenes mischief? Join my newsletter and never miss a thing.

What you'll get:

- New release alerts the moment a fresh cozy mystery or romance hits the shelves

- Exclusive freebies you won't find anywhere else

- Sneak peeks into works-in-progress

- Giveaways, gossip & goodies straight from my writing desk

- Early access to cover reveals, events, and special announcements

It's the easiest way to stay connected—and the only place where the real secrets are spilled.

https://www.pollyholmesmysteries.com/newsletter

Connect With Polly

Keep up to date on Polly's book releases, signings, and events on her website:
https://www.pollyholmesmysteries.com

Follow her on her Facebook page:
https://www.facebook.com/plharrisauthor/

Check out all the latest news in her Facebook group:
https://www.facebook.com/groups/magicmysteryroma nce

Follow her on her Instagram page:
https://www.instagram.com/plharris_pollyholmes_auth or/

Follow her on TikTok:
https://www.tiktok.com/@polly_holmes_author

Follow her on Amazon:
https://www.amazon.com/stores/Polly-Holmes/author/B07QNK9ZJJ

Follow her on Bookbub:

https://www.bookbub.com/authors/polly-holmes

Follow her on Goodreads:

https://www.goodreads.com/author/show/7558565.Polly_Holmes

ABOUT THE AUTHOR

Australian author Polly Holmes delights readers with paranormal and culinary cozy mysteries bursting with charm, mischief, and a dash of magic. Her stories blend action, humour, and unforgettable characters, creating page turning adventures that linger long after the final chapter.

When the clues turn darker and the stakes rise, she writes as P.L. Harris, delivering gripping paranormal and contemporary romances filled with heart pounding suspense and irresistible heat.

Both pen names belong to an internationally recognised, multi award-winning storyteller. Her work has been celebrated across the Daphne du Maurier Awards, the RWAus Ruby and Sapphire Awards, the Silver Falchion Awards, the Davitt Awards longlist, and numerous national business and literary honours.

When she's not conjuring mysteries or crafting romance, Polly can be found in her favourite café with a coffee in hand, rewatching classic whodunits, or strolling along the beach soaking up the salty Western Australian air.

For a complete list of her awards and accolade head on over to her website:

https://www.pollyholmesmysteries.com/media

The Cupcake Capers

Book One – Cupcakes and Cyanide

Welcome to Ashton Point. One sweet taste could be her last.

Charlotte McCorrson has spent her entire life building her business, CC's Simply Cupcakes. The town of Ashton Point is her home and she's garnered a reputation of stellar service and delightful pastries, one nibble at a time. But everything isn't as sweet in the sleepy, coastal town as Charlotte would like to think. She is in for a rude awakening and no amount of sugar will make this medicine go down any smoother.

After catering a large town-wide event, Ashton Point's morning newspaper fills Charlotte McCorrson with an icy sense of dread. The headlines scream Cupcake Killer! and put the blame squarely on CC's Simply Cupcakes. When bodies begin to pile up behind her confectionary goodies, Charlotte must prove that while her cupcakes are delicious, they aren't literally to die for—before she ends up in jail for a crime she didn't commit.

Follow the link below to continue reading the series through your favourite retailer.

<https://www.pollyholmesmysteries.com/the-cupcake-capers>

Read on for an excerpt of Cupcakes and Cyanide

Chapter one

"CALLING ALL THE single ladies."

Charlotte McCorrson stood nestled at the back of the reception centre, semi-hidden behind a burgundy-and-white, balloon topiary tree.

Great. Bouquet throwing time, just what I need. For every man in the room to know I'm still single.

When Beth invited her to the wedding she was over the moon, after all, they'd been good friends since Clair and her family moved to Ashton Point three years ago. What she hadn't planned on was still being single by the time the wedding rolled around.

They may as well take out a front-page ad in the Ashton Point Chronicle. She could see it now. "Ashton Point master cupcake baker extraordinaire struggles to snag herself a husband. Could she be lacking that special ingredient all men are looking for? What is wrong with the redheaded beauty?" She'd been over the moon when Beth and Lincoln asked CC's Simply Cupcakes to design a wedding cake, based around Charlotte's award-winning cupcake designs.

"Charlotte? What are you doing back here?" A petite voice spoke from behind.

She spun, her breath catching as her gaze landed on a vision in white. Decked out in a satin Karen Willis Holmes, floor-length, empire dress with embroidered tulle overlay, Beth was a vison of an angel. There had barely been a dry eye in the church as she walked down the aisle to her handsome prince. The fairy-tale wedding every bride dreams of.

Charlotte stiffened as Beth threw her arms around her neck and squeezed. "I never got a chance to properly thank you for the wonderful cupcake display you made. It was truly the cake of my dreams. I'm so glad you were able to share my special day with me. It wouldn't have been the same without you and Clair here," she said with a beaming smile.

"You're welcome, I wouldn't have missed it for the world. I'm so happy you liked it," Charlotte said in a muffled voice. Her mouth was half covered by blonde ruffles of hair, leaving the metallic taste of hairspray on her tongue.

Beth pulled back and their gazes held strong. "Liked it? Are you serious? I loved it." A bolt of electric energy ran up Charlotte's spine. She cherished the buzz she got from seeing the joy her cupcakes brought others. "And if anyone thinks they're taking the leftovers home tonight, they have another thing coming. That's all I'll be eating 'til we leave for our honeymoon next week."

Both ladies burst into laughter. Beth's happiness was starting to rub off on Charlotte.

"Didn't you hear the MC? You need to get to the dance floor. I'm about to throw the bouquet."

Charlotte cringed at the thought. "No, no, it's fine. I'm really okay sitting back and letting someone else take the limelight." She had planned on falling madly in love with the man of her dreams by the wedding.

I guess life doesn't always go to plan.

A sliver of disappointment marred Beth's expression. "I can't believe what I'm hearing. Your grandma would be turning in her grave if she knew you were skipping the bouquet toss. You know how she loved tradition."

Warmth filled Charlotte's heart. Her grandmother treasured her independence. She was the reason they'd moved to Ashton Point in the first place.

She shook her head. "I'm happy watching from the sidelines, besides, a mosh pit of single women jumping around like clucking chickens, all vying for their piece of the elusive dream isn't really my idea of fun."

"Now, that's something I'd like to see." A gruff voice echoed in her ear.

"Excuse me?" Charlotte said, spinning to see Lincoln's best man grinning like the Cheshire Cat.

"A mosh pit of single women jumping around like clucking chickens," he said with a cheeky grin. "Definitely something I'd pay money to see."

Beth sighed, rolled her eyes and play-punched him in the shoulder. "Give it a rest, Liam."

Liam… Mmmm. Why is it that all men named Liam are gorgeous? Liam Hemsworth, Liam Neeson.

Tanned, tall and handsome, he flashed a half smile at Charlotte and a spike of interest sparked in her belly.

Her gaze caught her sister, Clair, waving frantically behind Liam.

Saved by the bell.

"I'm sorry, Beth, but it looks like Clair needs me."

"Charlotte, there you are. I've been looking for you everywhere," Clair said as she joined them, flicking her deep-red ponytail over her shoulder.

"Why, is something wrong?" Alarm hit Charlotte square in the chest. "Please don't tell me we've run out of cupcakes? There should be plenty to go around. I made loads of extras."

Beth folded her arms across her chest and frowned. "Yes, don't tell me we ran out, otherwise the Bridezilla I've kept hidden inside might have to make a guest appearance."

"Bridezilla?" Liam said with a raised eyebrow. "I find that very hard to believe."

"When it comes to Charlotte's cupcakes, you better believe it," she snapped, holding his stern gaze in hers.

"Everyone calm down, there are plenty of cupcakes." Clair smiled and looped her arm through her sisters. "I was looking for Charlotte for the bouquet toss. Nothing better than a little competition between sisters.”

A grin spread across Beth’s face and she clapped her hands together. “Wonderful. I best go and get ready. Good luck,” Beth called over her shoulder as she hurried off.

“This should be a sight to see. I’ll let you two ladies get ready. I’d hate to be the one to keep you from your spot in the chicken brood,” Liam said with a smile as he strode back to the bridal table at the top of the dance floor.

Clair raised an eyebrow. “Chicken brood?”

“Never mind.” Charlotte shook her head.

“Wasn’t that the best man?” Clair asked, forcefully guiding Charlotte toward the crowded dance floor.

Charlotte nodded.

It certainly was THE best man.

She watched his retreating figure and her gaze seemed to have a mind of its own. It made its way down his broad shoulders, to his trim waist and tight derriere. Her cheeks grow hot as she imagined what he would look like out of his suit.

“What was his name again?” Clair’s words were met with silence. “Earth to Charlotte,” she said, flicking Charlotte’s forehead as if she were flicking a fly from the back of her hand. "What is his name?"

"Oww." Charlotte rubbed her forehead. "All right. I heard you the first time. Liam. His name is Liam."

Charlotte's stomach tightened as Clair elbowed their way to the centre of the dance floor dragging her along for the ride.

"Okay, ladies. Are we ready for the bouquet toss?" The deep, throaty voice of the MC blared out across the room.

Charlotte's body tensed as ear-splitting screams of single women pierced the air.

Oh my, could this be any more embarrassing?

To top it off, Beyoncé's *Single Ladies* boomed out as Beth took centre stage.

Charlotte's breath caught in her throat as her gaze snared Liam's sly grin from the front of the room.

What's with the grin?

Cheers erupted around her and her eyes widened as Beth's bouquet flew on a straight trajectory right into her arms.

* * *

Charlotte stood in the kitchen, her lungs void of air as the newspaper headline screamed at her like an unwanted nightmare. She held the morning newspaper in her icy fingers. *Cupcake Killer!*

Beth's wedding had been the event of the year, a perfect place to show off her culinary skills. The whole town had turned up to see her finally tie the knot with Lincoln Wade, Ashton Point's most eligible bachelor. Everyone who's anyone had been there, which meant more advertising for their business, CC's Simply Cupcakes.

"I don't believe this." Her hands shook as she read the front-page article. Definitely not the front page she had imagined last night at the wedding. "Why would they think *my* cupcakes killed someone?"

Her eyes were glued to the quote at the bottom of the page next to her picture.

Doctor says two beloved local councilmen are in critical condition and show signs of cyanide poisoning.

"Cyanide poisoning? What are they talking about?" she asked, collapsing on the kitchen stool as her knees gave way. "I do *not* cook with cyanide. Guests say that they began feeling ill after the cake was cut and cupcakes distributed."

Definitely not from my cupcakes.

Burning heat simmered in her veins. It was going to hit the fan, so to speak, when her sister, Clair, heard of this debacle. Thankfully Cassidy was over visiting Mum and Dad in New York for the next two weeks. *At least she won't be tarnished by this nightmare.*

This town was their home. They'd moved to Ashton Point on the central coast of New South Wales, just over three years ago to help her elderly grandma. "As if anyone would think I would intentionally poison someone. This is totally unfair," she said, slamming the paper down on the breakfast bar. Her stomach bottoming out as her gaze spotted the bouquet on the kitchen bench.

"What's unfair?" Clair asked, as she entered the kitchen.

Her sister's weary voice caught Charlotte off guard and her chest tightened like it was being forcibly crushed in a vice.

Damn it, there's no hiding this now.

She scooped up the newspaper before Clair spotted the disaster that was about to tear their dreams apart.

"What's unfair?" Clair repeated heading toward the Nespresso machine and wiping the crusty sleep remnants from the inner rim of her eyes.

Charlotte's pulse sped up. Clearing her throat, she stood and held the newspaper flat to her chest, ready to face the music head-on. "I've something to show you, but maybe you should get a coffee and sit down first." Clair was like a five-foot-five, grumpy bed monster with a toothache before her morning coffee.

"For goodness sake, Charlotte, spit it out," she said running her hand through her knotted hair. "I didn't exactly get much sleep last night, by the time we packed up after the wedding."

Charlotte cringed at the mention of the wedding. "You're going to hear about it one way or another." She sighed. "May as well be before you leave the house."

Clair's eyes narrowed and she leaned against the counter folding her arms across her chest. "Okay, enough with the cryptic clues and just tell me what you're talking about."

Charlotte's heart plummeted to the base of her gut. She flipped the paper around and held her breath. Waiting for the incoming explosion.

"Cupcake killer!" Clair's amused, bubbly giggle shot through Charlotte like a dagger. "That's ridiculous. We've known Daniel for three years and everyone in town knows he's big on sensationalising stories without getting his facts straight first. You're not taking that seriously, are you?"

"Of course I'm taking it seriously."

"It's just Daniel trying to big note his career. You and I know there's no truth to it and I'm sure when the truth is revealed, Daniel will be eating his own words." Clair busied herself working her mass of deep-red, bushy hair into a messy bun on the top of her head. "I'm sure it will blow over once they've worked out how they were really poisoned."

Charlotte's chest tightened. "I can't believe you're being so blasé about this. We've worked our butts off to make CC's Simply Cupcakes the best it can possibly be and…" She paused, fury running through her veins. She shook the newspaper in front of Clair's unimpressed expression. "…bad publicity is the last thing we need." Charlotte's stomach grumbled as the fresh scent of roasted hazelnut assaulted her nostrils.

Clair made two fresh cups and handed one off to Charlotte. "Okay, I suppose this isn't ideal, but I'd hardly think one article in the local rag is going to destroy our business. Besides, the whole town knows Daniel will bend the truth to sell one more newspaper."

Clair skimmed over the article. A myriad of emotions flashing across Clair's face made it impossible for Charlotte to determine her thoughts. "They say that no accusations will be acted upon until they have concrete evidence and they'll be following up all leads. Maybe we should keep our eyes and ears open, just in case."

Pain shot up from the base of Charlotte's neck and compounded her sudden headache into a dull roar. "I agree, but…"

Clair continued, brushing Charlotte's words aside. "And we have Mrs Stevenson's eightieth birthday high tea tomorrow afternoon, down by the river. I'm sure after that goes off without a hitch, Daniel will not only be eating his words, but also your delicious cupcakes."

"Maybe you're right, but I don't think we should wait for the fall out from this article. I know Beth was taking the leftovers home and I don't want her to worry, so I'm going to head over to reassure them that my cupcakes were not the source of the poisoning."

Clair fake coughed and her eyebrows shit up. "The morning after their wedding?"

Charlotte's pulse racing. Again. "They're not leaving for their honeymoon 'til Wednesday, and if I remember rightly, Lincoln has to work today to tie up loose ends before they leave."

She glanced one last time at the newspaper and huffed.

This is the most ludicrous thing ever put in print. I'll make you eat your words if it's the last thing I do.

Clair sighed. "Okay, but don't take too long. I'll be heading over to the shop soon to update the books and make sure we have enough supplies for Mrs Stevenson's order. I'll see you when you get there."

"Okay." Inside, she was furious at Clair's nonchalant attitude. "Mark my words, I'll get to the bottom of this."

* * *

Liam Bradly pressed his palms to the side of his head and squeezed his eyes shout. The incessant knocking on the door was an interruption to his morning breakfast he'd didn't need. He strutted toward the door. A continuous thunderous roar hammered his head, thanks to his addiction to good wine. He'd stupidly over-indulged at the wedding and his queasy stomach was a stark reminder of why he usually drank red instead of white wine.

He ran his hand through his hair and glanced at the wall clock. "Are you serious?" It's not even nine o'clock yet. Who the hell visits this early on a Saturday morning, especially after a late wedding reception the night before? He'd tear strips off whatever idiot was on the other side of the door.

Liam threw the oak door wide open. "Do you have any idea what time…" He froze mid-sentence, his eyes glued to the petite woman standing before him. He'd remember her anywhere. As if he'd forget a woman of her beauty. Her wavy red locks hung just below her shoulders, framing her face. This was much better than the semi-business look she'd worn yesterday at the wedding, hair pulled back in a tight bun. Now, she was the picture of a woman that would tantalise any man, including him.

She's beautiful.

A soft smile curved her lips, but her eyes told a different story. The drumming in his head shot his mind back to the present. He smiled. "Well, well, if it isn't the Cupcake Killer in person."

She gasped. "You read the article too?"

He nodded. "I'm sure everyone in town's read it. Hard not to see it. It was plastered all over the front page."

Her glossy, sapphire-blue eyes widened. Thrusting her hands on her hips she said, "That article is utter nonsense. They had no right to print it without any evidence. My cupcakes were not the reason those people got sick."

"Really?" he asked folding his arms across his chest giving her an uninterrupted view of his taut biceps and clenched abs.

Her jaw dropped to speak, but nothing came out. The only indication that she was still breathing was the warm, crimson blush that had worked its way from her neck to her cheeks.

"I…um… I wanted to…um…" She bit her bottom lip and paused mid-sentence as if her voice had suddenly vanished.

What the hell is with her eyes? Their constant flittering movement, combined with his throbbing head, was making him nauseous. It was as if she didn't know where to look.

He was standing there in only his pyjama bottoms with the door wide open for the whole neighbourhood to see. A rush of triumph surged through his system.

Nice to know my body can still affect a woman that way.

He gestured toward his lack of attire. "My apologies, I wasn't expecting visitors," he said as he waved her inside. "Come in while I get something more appropriate on."

She shook her head. "I'm fine. I just wanted to speak to Beth, if she was around."

Liam turned and headed back inside. "Happy to chat after I get dressed. Close the door after you come in, will you?"

He hurriedly dressed and walked into the kitchen, half expecting the red-headed beauty not to be there. But there she was, standing in front of the sliding glass door framed by the morning glow of the sun. She looked naturally beautiful in a quiet, understated way.

He shoved his hands in his trouser pockets. "Don't tell me…you've decided to cook me breakfast. I'm not sure my stomach can handle one of your delicious cyanide cupcakes this morning."

She spun and stared straight through him. It unnerved him. Colour leached from her face, leaving her white as a sheet. Stepping back, she stumbled. Liam let out a string of curses as he lunged for her before she face-planted on the kitchen tiles.

"I'm sorry. That was meant to be a joke. Obviously in poor taste," he said, still holding her elbow and refusing to let go until he was sure she had both feet planted firmly on the ground. Liam rubbed the elbow he'd grabbed, trying to alleviate any discomfort he may have caused by his firm grip.

"Yes, poor taste, indeed," she said huskily, easing her arm from his hold.

"It seems we were both rather busy at the wedding yesterday, and after your triumph in the bouquet toss, you disappeared. We never got the chance to formally meet." He held his hand out, eager for the introduction. "I'm Liam Bradly."

She looked at him in bewilderment, as if he were speaking gibberish, then stepped back and thrust her hand out in his direction, clearly determined to keep him at arms-length. "Charlotte McCorrson."

He smiled and shook her hand. "Nice to meet you, Charlotte." His hand pulsed under her warm touch. A soft smile curved her lips, her eyes glittering under the morning sun.

She withdrew her hand from his grip. "I didn't know you were staying here. I actually came over to see Beth. I wanted to reassure her my cakes were not the source of the poisoning and that article is utter garbage."

"Well, as you can see she's not here, or Lincoln for that matter. They left for their honeymoon in the early hours of this morning, but I'm sure they wouldn't believe it anyway."

"Oh," she said anxiously. "I thought they weren't leaving 'til Wednesday?"

"My surprise wedding gift," Liam said. It was the least he could do for his best friend.

"Are you house-sitting for them?" Her eyebrows went up in question.

House-sitting?

The thought would have most certainly filled him with dread. That was before he met Charlotte. Now the idea had merit.

I have holidays due, and Lincoln did say to make myself at home before they left. A week relaxing in this quiet town, getting to know the locals, one in particular, was definitely preferable to heading back to Perth to his mundane job of counting numbers on people's tax returns.

"Yes, I'll be house-sitting while they're on their honeymoon. Maybe you can show me around town while I'm here," he said flashing his cheekiest smile.

She gave him a peculiar look, apprehension entering her gaze. She shook her head. "I'm sorry, I can't. I have to get to the bottom of this poisoning before my entire business is ruined."

"Why would someone want to ruin your business?" he pried.

Her hands clenched and she let out a sigh. "As if I would know. It's not like we have enemies in town. I'm sure it's all a big misunderstanding."

He was up for an adventure. "Maybe we could make a deal. You show me around town and I'll help you solve the mystery of the cyanide bandit, what do you say?"

Charlotte froze, and her skin flushed. She hastily moved past him and headed for the door. "I'm sorry, I can't. Enjoy your stay in Ashton Point."

Book Two – Cupcakes and Curses

Murder and cupcakes, a deadly mix.
Clair McCorrson has spent the last three years building her business, CC's Simply Cupcakes with her sister gaining a

reputation for mouth-watering excellence in their seaside town of Ashton Point. While Charlotte is the master baker, Clair keeps the business side looking sweet and if everything goes as planned, she'll be more than the girl behind the scenes.

Expanding their business to the nearby town of Watson's Creek is Clair's idea, and acquiring the Sweets Mansion is her dream come true, her chance to step out from her sister's shadow and make it on her own. Clair's excitement quickly turns sour when she stumbles across the murdered body of local settlement agent.

Newspaper headlines screaming Cupcake Killer Strikes Again! Clair's life seems to be going from bad to worse when rumours of the cursed Mansion begin to surface igniting chaos among the locals. Bodies literally begin to mount up around CC's Simply Cupcakes and all the evidence points to Clair. Wrongly accused of murder, it's a race against time to find the real culprit before she spends the rest of her life behind bars.

Book Three – Cupcakes and Corpses
When it comes to design, death is in the details.

Cassidy McCorrson has worked hard to develop her reputation as a leading interior designer in her seaside town of Ashton Point. Since arriving home from visiting her parents in New York, her skills have been in high demand. Between juggling the design for her sister's new cupcake shop and her private client, Cassidy barely has time to prepare for the upcoming Christmas celebrations.

Cassidy is excited at the prospect of delivering designs she can be proud of, but her world is turned upside down when the body of a local reporter is found murdered on location at her latest work site. What should have been a straightforward job turns out to be the worst decision of her life.

In order to clear her name and restore her reputation, Cassidy must find the real killer before she ends up redesigning the interior of a jail cell. Can she unearth the killer before time runs out?

Book Four – Mistletoe and Murder

Mistletoe magic or the kiss of death?

Alexandra Cohen is determined to show her boss she has what it takes to be manager of The Springs Café on the outskirts of Ashton Point. She's smart and with the addition of CC's Simply Cupcakes, sales have sky-rocketed. The town is in full holiday spirit and with the Christmas Fair fast approaching, Alex has to work twice as hard to keep her interfering ex-boyfriend, out of the picture before he destroys her life forever.

After reluctantly agreeing to run the kissing booth at the fair, Alex has to deal with a continuous line of male customers, as well as an ex who has ignored her requests to leave her alone. But the day is really tarnished when Alex stumbles across a body on the ground of her kissing booth dressed as Santa. The evidence is gathering against her and Alex must decide if she should let the police do their job and pray they do it well or if she should take matters into her own hands. With the help of the McCorrson sisters, Alex must investigate so she doesn't become the town scapegoat and forced to spend Christmas behind bars.

Book Five – Dead Velvet Cupcakes

A stab at the competition.

Since arriving in Ashton Point, Master Chef Margarete Becker has managed to turn the dilapidated, old Tea 4 Two Café into a thriving meeting place. She draws both locals and tourists with her mouth-watering treats. Her childhood dream is to own her own 5-star restaurant and with the success of the Tea 4 Two Café, that dream could become a reality sooner than she imagined.

Margarete's chance to show she has what it takes to run not just a café, but a thriving restaurant arrives when she secures the contract to cater the McCorrson's 30th Wedding Anniversary dinner. With dessert taken care of, Margarete's has only the entrée and main course to perfect. A piece of cake…or so she thought. It proves a slice more difficult than expected when the body of a local chef, Margarete's competition, is found murdered.

Evidence against Margarete is mounting and it's obvious someone is trying to frame her. She only has one option; enlist the help of the McCorrson sisters to help clear her name and find the real killer before time runs out and her dreams are shattered forever.

www.ingramcontent.com/pod-product-compliance
Lightning Source LLC
Chambersburg PA
CBHW031316060726

47590CB00003B/1233